The Immigrant Experience

The Immigrant Experience

Kremena Spengler

Living in AMERICA

CREATIVE EDUCATION
CREATIVE PAPERBACKS

Published by Creative Education and Creative Paperbacks
P.O. Box 227, Mankato, Minnesota 56002
Creative Education and Creative Paperbacks are imprints
of The Creative Company
www.thecreativecompany.us

Book design by Graham Morgan (www.bluedes.com)
Art direction by Tom Morgan
Edited by Jill Kalz

Images by Getty (Andrew Lichtenstein, Bettmann, Gerardo Vieyra/NurPhoto, John Autey / MediaNews Group / St. Paul Pioneer Press, Mario Tama, Victor J. Blue/Bloomberg), Unsplash (Barbara Zandoval, Joel Naren, Miko Guziuk, Should Wang), Wikimedia Commons (Amyyfory, Detroit Publishing Co., DFID - UK Department for International Development, Donna Burton, Dorothea Lange, Ferdinand Schmutzer, Joseph Keppler, New York Public Library, William Halsall)

Library of Congress Cataloging-in-Publication Data
Names: Spengler, Kremena, author.
Title: The immigrant experience / by Kremena Spengler.
Description: Mankato, Minnesota : Creative Education, Creative Paperbacks, [2025] | Series: Living in America | Includes webography. | Includes bibliographical references and index. | Audience: Ages 12–15 years | Audience: Grades 7–9 | Summary: "A social studies title for young adults that examines the history of immigration in the United States of America and how immigrants affect the economy and society. Includes sidebars, real-person profiles, a glossary, a timeline, and further resources"—Provided by publisher.
Identifiers: LCCN 2023046983 (print) | LCCN 2023046984 (ebook) | ISBN 9781640269125 (library binding) | ISBN 9781682774625 (paperback) | ISBN 9798889890805 (ebook)
Subjects: LCSH: United States—Emigration and immigration—History—Juvenile literature. | United States—Emigration and immigration—Government policy—Juvenile literature. | United States—Emigration and immigration—Social aspects—Juvenile literature. | United States—Emigration and immigration—Public opinion—Juvenile literature. | Immigrants—United States—Social conditions—Juvenile literature. | Immigrants—United States—Economic conditions—Juvenile literature.
Classification: LCC JV6450 .S74 2025 (print) | LCC JV6450 (ebook) | DDC 305.9/069120973—dc23/eng/20231219
LC record available at https://lccn.loc.gov/2023046983
LC ebook record available at https://lccn.loc.gov/2023046984

Printed in China

LLEGAL

THE UNITED ST

ORIGINAL
TO BE GIVEN TO
THE PERSON NATURALIZED

CERTIFICATE OF

Petition No. 6410

Personal description of holder as of date of naturaliza
complexion light ; color of eyes brown
weight 128 pounds; visible distinctive marks no
Marital status Unmarried
I certify that the description above given is tr

sign here

UNITED STATE
EASTERN DIST
Be it k
Ea
held pursua
on Janu
ENG
then residing

CONTENTS

Introduction

From 2003 to 2005, the government of Sudan deliberately killed 200,000 civilians in the region of Darfur. Another two million people were forced out of their homes. Makka Djibrine Khatir's parents fled to Chad to save their family. Makka's mother, pregnant with Makka and her twin sister, rode a donkey. Makka's grandmother walked alongside.

Makka was born in a refugee camp in Chad. The family lived there for 12 years. Makka and her seven siblings attended school in the camp. The school had harsh discipline, and Makka was afraid of the teachers. One day, Makka missed school to take her sick brother to the hospital. Afterward, she was taken to the principal's office. The principal beat her with a whip. Her back bled.

In 2015, Makka and her family were accepted by the United States as refugees. They were resettled in Buffalo, New York. Makka entered seventh grade at a middle school for recent immigrants. She did not know a word of English. Because of her past experiences in the refugee camp, she was afraid of the teachers. But the teachers wanted to help her. She was shocked when a teacher tried to give her a hug.

Makka's new school changed her life. She graduated with the highest honors. As of 2023, she was a straight-A student at Buffalo State University, majoring in International Relations.

For people like Makka, the United States is a land of refuge and opportunity. They get a new start. In turn, they shape the nation with their own hard work and unique traditions.

A cartoon from 1880 depicts Uncle Sam "saving" immigrants by welcoming them to the United States.

CHAPTER 1:

Waves of Immigrants

Everyone in the United States is either an immigrant or the descendant of one. Even American Indians. Their ancestors arrived from Asia thousands of years ago. Those prehistoric people crossed a land bridge from what is now Siberia to Alaska.

European immigration to the Americas began after Christopher Columbus landed in the New World in 1492. Spain, France, Great Britain, the Netherlands, and Sweden set up outposts in North America. The 13 British **colonies** along the Atlantic coast would one day form the United States. Some colonists came in search of economic opportunities. Others wanted the freedom to practice their faith. In 1620, about 100 Pilgrims fled religious **persecution** in Great Britain. They started a colony in Plymouth, Massachusetts. A larger religious group, the Puritans, set up the

Massachusetts Bay Colony. About 20,000 Puritans migrated to this region between 1630 and 1640.

Some colonists were forced immigrants. They came as **indentured servants**. They were forced into years of free labor. Many British prisoners were also forcibly shipped to the colonies. However, the biggest group of forced immigrants were not servants but enslaved people. The earliest records of slavery in America include 20 Africans forced into slavery in Jamestown in 1619. By 1680, there were about 7,000 Africans in the colonies. By 1790, their number had swelled to 700,000.

The first U.S. **census** in 1790—which excluded American Indians—put the U.S. population at 3.9 million. About 80 percent were white, and about 20 percent were of African origin. While most settlers were British and blended into the dominant culture, ethnic tension still happened. In 1751, Benjamin Franklin worried that the Germans of Pennsylvania would "Germanize us." Some historians call this the first ethnic crisis in U.S. history.

Wars in Europe and the United States slowed immigration from 1789 to 1815. But people immigrated in full force when peace came. The first major wave of immigration started in the 1840s. It included mass arrivals from Ireland and Germany. Two events drove it. A potato crop failure caused a **famine** in Ireland. It killed one million people. Desperate families fled to the United States. Young Germans rebelled against their government in 1848. They were defeated and had to flee.

Nearly half of all immigrants in the 1840s were Irish. Between 1820 and 1860, the Irish made up one-third of all immigrants to the United States. They settled at first in New York and Boston,

The Pilgrims came to America in 1620 aboard the *Mayflower*, all looking for better lives.

ZOOM IN: ELLIS ISLAND

Ellis Island began receiving immigrants in 1892. Annie Moore, a teenage girl from Ireland, made history as the first person to be processed there. The enormous station housed inspection facilities, hospitals, cafeterias, railroad ticket offices, and more. First- and second-class passengers were not inspected. They were not believed likely to become a burden or threat. Third-class passengers, who traveled at the bottom of crowded, dirty steamships, were inspected. Each ship's log contained the immigrant's name and answers to 29 questions. It was used to cross-examine the immigrant. The process lasted three to five hours. More than 12 million people entered the United States through Ellis Island between 1892 and 1954.

Massachusetts. Many took unskilled jobs in factories. Some moved west with construction crews. Most Irish immigrants were Catholic and poor. They were not easily accepted. Their presence gave rise to the first **nativist** movement in the United States, the "Know-Nothings." The nativists were against immigration. Violent mobs burned down a Catholic church in New York City. Riots in Philadelphia, Pennsylvania, left 13 dead. The nativists even formed a political party. It gained some seats in government but failed to win the presidency.

In the 1800s, about five million Germans made the United States their home. Many made their way into the Midwest, buying farms or working as skilled craftsmen. Germans brought their customs, music, and food to cities such as Chicago, Illinois; Milwaukee, Wisconsin; and St. Louis, Missouri. The defeated German rebels were university scholars. They debated politics, published newspapers, and participated in organized sports.

Immigration decreased during the Civil War (1861–1865). But afterward, people were needed to fill jobs. The nation was expanding west. U.S. states sent agents to Europe to find new settlers. Railroad companies offered immigrants reduced fares. In the next few decades, the Germans and the Irish were joined by the Swedes, Norwegians, and Danes. These Scandinavians settled in Wisconsin, Minnesota, and the Dakotas, finding places that reminded them of home.

It was not until 1875 that the U.S. government began to restrict immigration. The Immigration Act of 1875 (the Page Act) barred criminals, forced laborers from Asia, and Chinese women from coming into the country. An 1882 law barred "convicts," "lunatics," and "idiots." That law set a 50-cent fee for new arrivals.

Ellis Island was the portal for the ancestors of about 40 percent of today's Americans.

The California Gold Rush of 1848 had brought about 25,000 Chinese immigrants. They worked in the gold mines, clothing factories, farms, and on railroads. Although they made up a tiny 0.002 percent of the U.S. population, whites blamed them for low wages. In 1882, Congress passed the Chinese Exclusion Act. It banned Chinese laborers from entering the country for 10 years. This ban was later made permanent. The law also denied citizenship to people of Chinese descent. It was the first law in U.S. history to target an entire ethnic group. The ban on Chinese immigration was not lifted until 1943.

Between 1880 and 1914, more than 20 million immigrants arrived in the United States. The foreign-born population peaked at 14.8 percent in 1890. But while the previous generations had come from northern and western Europe, the majority this time came from its south and east. People poured in from countries such as Italy, Russia, Poland, and Greece. In the 1850s, only 1 percent of immigrants were from southern or eastern Europe. By the 1880s, their share had risen to 20 percent. By 1910, it was 70 percent. By 1920, when immigration began to subside, more than four million Italians had arrived. About three million Jews made the journey between 1880 and 1924. This wave was driven by changes on both sides of the Atlantic Ocean. The United States was quickly becoming urban and industrialized. But many parts of Europe remained rural and poor. Violence, diseases, land shortages, and unemployment were common. Transatlantic travel became more affordable. Word of American riches and success came from returning immigrants and U.S. agents.

When immigrants arrived in the United States, they were processed through government immigration centers. More than 70

ZOOM IN: GERMAN AMERICANS IN WWI

World War I fueled anti-German feelings in the United States. The institutions of German Americans came under attack. The names of foods, streets, and towns were changed. German-language newspapers were run out of business or closed quietly. German-language books were burned. Americans who spoke German were threatened with violence. German-language classes in schools were discontinued and, in some places, outlawed. Some German Americans reacted by defending their loyalty to the United States. Some changed the names of their businesses and even their own names. The long German language and literature tradition in the United States never fully recovered.

Riots targeting German Americans broke out in 1915 in opposition to Germany's role in WWI.

percent entered through New York City, which became known as the "Golden Door." The busiest processing center was Ellis Island. It opened in New York Harbor in 1892.

Many of the new immigrants were qualified only for unskilled, dangerous jobs in cities. In 1890, nearly 90 percent of the laborers in New York's Department of Public Works were Italian immigrants. They dug canals, laid paving and gas lines, built bridges, and tunneled out the New York subway system. Immigrant women and children toiled in dark, unsafe factories. In one example, a fire broke out at the Triangle Shirtwaist factory in New York in 1911. It killed 146 workers, nearly half of them young Italian women.

Many immigrants in large cities lived in narrow, crowded apartment buildings. These buildings had poor lighting and ventilation. People fell victim to easily spread diseases. But the immigrants also

BROS.
BANCA MALZONE

created lively neighborhoods, with restaurants, banks, and shops. They took up trades such as shoemaking, stonework, and barbering. They set up mutual-aid societies and libraries. In time, they shared in the broader success of earlier Americans.

As immigration peaked, so did pushback against it. Immigrants were blamed again for taking American jobs. The press often promoted theories that Asians and "Mediterranean types" were lesser people than northern Europeans. Drawings and songs mocked them as childlike, criminal, or subhuman. Anti-immigrant groups damaged and destroyed immigrant churches and charities. In the 1890s alone, more than 20 Italians were hanged.

Public feelings brought new legal restrictions on immigration. In the early 1900s, Congress passed laws that banned political extremists, people with disabilities, and people from Japan. In 1917, it banned immigration from much of Asia and the Middle East. It made new arrivals take a literacy test. The Emergency **Quota** Act of 1921 and the Immigration Act of 1924 (the Johnson-Reed Act) set immigration limits based on nationality. The quotas heavily favored people of northern and western European origin. Just three countries—Great Britain, Ireland, and Germany—were assigned 70 percent of all the immigration slots. Immigration from southern and eastern Europe was reduced. Asians were excluded. World War I (1914–18) and the Great Depression (1929–39) also reduced immigration.

But World War II brought about labor shortages. U.S. men joined the armed forces or left farms to work in factories in support of the war effort. In response, the government brought in farm workers from Mexico. By the time the Bracero Program ended in 1964, it had brought five million Mexican workers into the country.

The Immigration and Nationality Act of 1952 (the McCarran-Walter Act) replaced the previous laws. It changed the quota calculations, but it kept the nationality quotas in place. This law ended the ban on immigration from Asia.

Walls along the southern U.S. border are meant to deter unauthorized immigration from Mexico.

CHAPTER 2:

A Modern System Develops

The quota system formed the basis of U.S. immigration policy for 40 years. Things changed with the Immigration and Nationality Act of 1965 (the Hart-Cellar Act). This law stressed uniting families and attracting skilled labor over national origin.

The law also regulated immigration from the Western Hemisphere for the first time. It set numerical caps. The caps were not intended to keep some ethnic groups out. Rather, they were meant to prevent any one group from dominating immigration. The law assigned 170,000 total immigration **visas** a year to countries in the Eastern Hemisphere and 120,000 to the Western Hemisphere. Each country received up to 20,000 slots.

The tide of immigration turned away from Europe. Most immigrants began arriving from Asia and Latin America. In the decade after the Immigration and Nationality Act of 1965 passed, the biggest source countries of immigration were Mexico, Cuba, the Philippines, and Italy. For the first time, the law

BIENVENIDOS
LOS
TRABAJADORES
MEXICANOS
BRACEROS
MEXICANOS
VIVAN
MEXICO

ZOOM IN: BRACERO PROGRAM

In 1942, the United States and Mexico created the Bracero Program. *Bracero* means "laborer" in Spanish. The program allowed Mexican men to work legally in the United States on short-term contracts. It helped ease a shortage of farm labor during World War II. The braceros were paid little. They were overcharged for room and board and exposed to harmful chemicals. The program was very popular with U.S. farmers and did not end until 1964. More than five million Mexicans came to the United States as braceros, and hundreds of thousands stayed on. The program resulted in an influx of authorized and unauthorized workers.

Most legal guest workers called braceros were transported from Mexico by train or airplane to jobs in the States.

created a special category for refugees and asylum seekers. After the Vietnam War, large numbers of refugees from Southeast Asia fled to the United States. Of about 800,000 U.S. immigrants in 1980, about 150,000 came from Vietnam, Laos, and Cambodia. About 125,000 were Cubans who asked for political asylum. The government set up resettlement programs for the refugees.

As Mexico became the largest source country for legal admissions, it also became the largest origin for unauthorized immigrants. By the mid-1980s, three to five million people were living unlawfully in the United States. The Immigration Reform and Control Act of 1986 (IRCA) attempted to fix this issue. On the one hand, IRCA allowed most unauthorized immigrants already in the country to apply for legal status. On the other hand, the law penalized employers who hired unauthorized immigrants. It increased funding for border enforcement. The law created a category for temporary, seasonal farm workers. But it did not raise the caps. The demand for workers remained higher than supply.

In contrast, the Immigration Act of 1990 raised the caps for legal immigration. It tried to ease entry for highly skilled workers. This law also created protections for people fleeing wars or natural disasters. It started a diversity visa lottery. The lottery randomly grants 50,000 immigrant visas each year to applicants from countries with low rates of immigration.

In 1996, Congress tightened immigration rules. It became easier to detain and deport immigrants without a hearing. People were barred from the country for smaller reasons than in the past. Some groups of legal immigrants lost access to federal benefits such as Medicaid and food stamps. Unauthorized immigrants were barred from any kind of federal benefits. The laws made it possible to track foreign visitors. These provisions would become part of the national security strategy after September 11, 2001. On that day, 19 Islamic terrorists hijacked 4 airplanes and carried out suicide attacks in New York City and Washington, D.C. Almost 3,000 people were killed. The terrorists had arrived in the United States legally, even though some of them were on watchlists. The public wanted to know why. The immigration issue was linked to national security.

In 2002, the government started collecting fingerprints from foreign-born Muslims. This program was later expanded to collect similar data from all foreigners entering the country. Another law required states to check immigration status before issuing a driver's license. A 2006 law provided for the construction of 700 miles (1,100 kilometers) of fence along the nation's southern border.

Federal agents worked with local authorities to increase arrests of unauthorized immigrants. Immigrant supporters pushed back. In response, some local governments passed **sanctuary** policies. These policies limited how much local police could cooperate with the federal government on enforcement, especially in California, Illinois, and New Jersey.

Several immigration reform attempts failed in the early 2000s. Some lawmakers favored a strict policy. They stressed border security and enforcement of current laws. Others wanted to increase legal immigration and to enable unauthorized immigrants to remain in the country legally. These disagreements made it impossible to make needed changes in Congress. As a result, presidents have responded with executive orders. Presidential orders do not require the approval of Congress. In 2012, President Barack Obama created the Deferred Action for Childhood Arrivals (DACA) program. It shielded unauthorized immigrants who had been brought to the United States as children from being

In addition to motor vehicles, horses are used to patrol the southern U.S. border because they're quick and quiet.

deported. But it did not provide a path to citizenship for these so-called "Dreamers."

Obama's successor, President Donald Trump, used presidential powers to reduce immigration in many ways. He called for the construction of a wall along the entire border with Mexico. He redirected Pentagon funds meant for U.S. defense to do it. In 2017, Trump banned travel from six Muslim countries. He brought back a deportation program ended by Obama. He put penalties on sanctuary cities that sheltered undocumented immigrants. In 2018, he started a zero-tolerance policy. Everyone who crossed the border without authorization was arrested. Children were separated from their parents and placed in different facilities. The family separations drew concern and condemnation from people across the country. The Trump administration also started the Remain in Mexico program. It required asylum seekers to wait in Mexico while their cases were pending in U.S. courts. According to immigrant supporters, this placed many vulnerable people at the mercy of gangs and corrupt officials across the border.

ZOOM IN: IMMIGRANTS AND CRIME

Some people say unauthorized immigrants are breaking the law simply by being in the United States without permission. This is correct. However, the law considers it a civil, not a criminal, offense. In 2017, the Migration Policy Institute estimated that a mere 2.7 percent of the 11 million unauthorized immigrants had committed a serious crime of some sort. This compared to 6 percent of the general population. According to a 2015 study by the National Academies of Sciences, Engineering, and Medicine, foreign-born men ages 18 to 39 are jailed at one-fourth the rate of native-born men of the same ages.

In 2020, many countries closed their borders because of the COVID-19 pandemic. The Trump administration used the health emergency to turn away asylum seekers. It also suspended the processing of many immigrant and temporary work visas.

President Joe Biden also used his powers to influence immigration. He lifted travel bans, resumed visa processing, and stopped

Some parts of the border wall between Mexico and the United States are made of steel, while others are wood or concrete.

construction of the border wall. The Biden administration expanded the list of countries whose citizens can stay in the United States because their countries are not safe.

Scholars say there are limits to presidents solving immigration issues without Congress. Presidents can act only within existing law. Their actions are likely to get challenged in court, sometimes by individual states. This increases tension between the federal and state governments. Policies change every time the White House changes hands.

CHAPTER 3:

Immigrants Today

The U.S. immigration system is organized around four goals: reuniting families, filling labor needs, protecting refugees, and promoting diversity. About two-thirds of all immigrants arrive to join their families. About one-fifth are supported, or sponsored, by employers. The rest are refugees, diversity visa recipients, and groups such as Afghans or Iraqis who worked with the U.S. government.

Since the 1990s, the United States has been admitting more than one million new legal immigrants each year. The cap is 675,000, but the spouses, parents, and children of U.S. citizens are admitted outside the cap. Demand for immigrant visas (called **green cards**) is far greater than supply. Many workers come on temporary visas and hope to change their status and stay. Temporary categories include seasonal farm work and highly skilled technical jobs. One program allows international students to work in the United States for a year or two after graduation from a U.S. university.

As of 2022, becoming a naturalized U.S. citizen took an average of 7.2 years

ZOOM IN: GAIN OR DRAIN

In 2019, the Cato Institute studied programs such as Social Security (retirement benefits), Medicare (health care for the elderly), Medicaid (health care for people with low incomes), food stamps, school lunches, cash payments, rental assistance, and food assistance for mothers with young children. It found that immigrants cost much less than the native-born in every program except the smallest one (food assistance for mothers with young children). The cost of a native-born mother to this program was $19 per person in 2019. The cost of an immigrant mother was $21, just $2 more per year.

To qualify as a refugee, a person must prove fear of persecution because of their race, political opinion, social group, or nationality. Asylum is available for the same reasons but to persons who are already in the United States. Asylum rules have become stricter in recent years.

The United States has more immigrants than any other country. They numbered 45.3 million in 2021, which is 13.6 percent of the population. They made up 17 percent of the workforce. While previous waves of immigrants were primarily from Europe, now most immigrants come from Latin America and Asia. In 2021, 44 percent of the immigrants identified as Hispanic and 27 percent as Asian. In fact, since 2009, more Asians have been arriving than Hispanics. Asians are expected to surpass Hispanics in number by 2065.

Mexicans are still the largest single ethnic group (24 percent) in the United States, but their share is decreasing. Other big groups are people from India (6 percent) and China (5 percent). Many others are from the Philippines, South Korea, and Central American countries.

Descendents of immigrants from Italy still celebrate the traditions of their European ancestors.

Immigrants now are much better educated than immigrants in the past. This is especially true of newer arrivals and of East Asians. In 2021, 71 percent of East Asian immigrants aged 25 and older had a college degree.

More than half of all immigrants live in just four states: California, Texas, Florida, and New York. But since the 1990s, new arrivals have spread out across the country to take jobs in farming, food processing, and construction. Some small states in the Midwest, West, and South have had their immigrant populations triple in size. Some communities have been very welcoming. Others have been less friendly. Places without a history of immigration are not always prepared to welcome large new groups. Some of them lack sufficient housing and other services to help people from new cultures. Schools have no programs for English learners, for example. As a result, some communities pass policies to restrict immigrants.

Most immigrants are legal. But nearly one-fourth (23 percent) are unauthorized. The unauthorized group more than tripled from 1990 to 2007, then leveled off. In 2019, the Migration Policy Institute estimated that 11 million unauthorized immigrants lived in this country. Two-thirds of them were from Mexico and Central America, 15 percent from Asia, and smaller groups were from the rest of the world. The number of unauthorized

In the 1990s, thousands of Haitian refugees sought protection in U.S. waters aboard overcrowded boats.

Mexicans has decreased by two million since 2007, but groups from Asia and Central America are increasing.

Contrary to some beliefs, not all unauthorized immigrants secretly cross the southern border. Many come into the country legally, then overstay their visas. The Migration Policy Institute says that from 2010 to 2017, overstayers outnumbered border crossers 2 to 1. They now make up 42 percent of unauthorized immigrants. Still, attempts to cross the southern border spiked to 2.4 million in 2022, from a previous peak of 1.6 million in 2000. The surge was driven by people from nations such as Cuba, Nicaragua, Venezuela, Haiti, Honduras, and El Salvador. The COVID-19 pandemic crippled the economies of these countries. Desperate migrants fled food shortages, gang violence, and other disasters.

In the past, border crossers were mostly young men looking for jobs. Now, many are families with children or even children traveling alone. Their goal is to seek asylum in the United States. This change brings new challenges to the country. The U.S. border strategy was designed to stop single adults. It centers around criminal charges, fast removal, and holding facilities. These

ZOOM IN: DESPERATION AND DIVISION

May 2023 was a desperate time in U.S. immigration history. COVID-19 pandemic rules that had helped people out were expiring. Officials processed more than 10,000 arrivals at the U.S. border with Mexico each day that month, the highest levels ever. Border facilities were holding thousands of migrants, far beyond their capacity. People huddled on sidewalks in border towns. The governors of Florida and Texas, who favored strict control of unauthorized immigration, shipped busloads of migrants into sanctuary cities such as Chicago and New York.

sequences are difficult to apply to families and children. In May 2023, border processing centers and shelters overflowed. Asylum cases were backed up in the courts. The U.S. asylum backlog neared a record 1.6 million at the end of 2022. The average wait time for an asylum hearing was about 4.3 years.

Local, state, and federal policies treat unauthorized immigrants differently. Some states issue driver's licenses to them. Some states offer in-state rates of tuition to public universities and even some health coverage from state funds. Sanctuary cities guarantee shelter. They refuse to help federal authorities arrest unauthorized immigrants. But other states and cities are strict in checking legal status. They forbid renting housing to the unauthorized or hiring them for work.

Regardless of their status, newcomers face challenges as they adjust to life in the United States. There may be an inability to communicate. According to the Pew Research Center, as of 2021, nearly half (46 percent) of immigrants knew little or no English. It affects their ability to get health care and other services, deal with the government or insurance companies, and understand legal documents. It is a barrier in the workplace, too. Poor English is a common reason to struggle to find a job. Even a foreign accent can slow advancement at work. Immigrants lacking solid language skills are easy prey for scams. For example, in 2020, the Internal Revenue Service (IRS) reported a scam that targeted people with poor English. The scammers asked for personal and financial information, threatening jail and deportation if their demands weren't met.

The language issue affects not only immigrants but also their children. From a young age, children are called on to translate or make phone calls for parents. Learning to switch between languages and cultures can be stressful and confusing. Immigrant parents may lack cultural knowledge and social connections. This makes it more difficult to guide their children about school, college applications, or budgeting.

Some immigrants deal with trauma. They may have experienced violence in their home country or on their journey to the United States. Women and girls, especially, are at increased risk of abuse and trafficking.

Skilled and highly educated immigrants, such as doctors or teachers, may find it hard to continue their careers. Licenses and other credentials may be difficult to transfer to the United States. These professionals may take low-skilled jobs quickly to support their families. It can bring feelings of loss or low self-worth. It can affect their family's ability to save for college or retirement.

Regardless of barriers, studies do find that immigrants today blend into American society as well as immigrants in the past. The immigrants share American values, such as hard work and patriotism. Their children achieve similar outcomes as other Americans in areas such as education, earnings, and housing.

CHAPTER 4:

The Impact of Immigrants

Picture life without pizza. Or without the computer search engine Google. These, and many other wonderful things, are the work of immigrants! Pizza arrived in the United States in the early 20th century.

It came along with the wave of Italians who settled in the large cities of the Northeast. Sergey Brin, who emigrated from the Soviet Union with his family at age six, co-founded Google with Larry Page. He became one of the richest people in the world.

Immigration has touched every part of American life. It has shaped the nation's identity and transformed its culture and politics. Immigrants have helped build and grow the world's largest economy. They have revitalized both large cities and small rural communities. In some inner cities, their presence has helped stop urban decay and violent crime. They have slowed

Immigrants bring their home-country flavors to the greater American dinner table.

ZOOM IN: TOO MANY TO NAME

Did you know that two of the most "American" songs, "God Bless America" and "White Christmas," are the works of an immigrant? Composer Irving Berlin was born as Israel Baline in Russia. Many of the most influential cultural figures in the United States were born outside the country. They range from inventors such as Alexander Graham Bell, Wernher von Braun, Igor Sikorsky, and Elon Musk, to Hollywood greats such as Frank Capra, Alfred Hitchcock, and Samuel Goldwyn. Pop culture stars include Justin Bieber, Drake, Van Halen, Shakira, Gal Gadot, and more. One immigrant name is a synonym for "genius"—the German-born physicist Albert Einstein.

Scientific genius Albert Einstein emigrated from Germany in 1933 and became a U.S. citizen in 1940.

or reversed population decline in countless small towns and sometimes even rescued them from dying.

Social scientists say immigration has changed the face of the United States—*literally*. For much of the 20th century, race was mainly a matter of Black and white. In 1960, 85 percent of Americans were white. When most of them thought of minorities, they pictured Black people. Immigration created a much more diverse society. It changed how Americans think about race. It changed the very words they use to talk about race. The term "model minority" was attached to East Asians. The word "Hispanic" was rarely used 50 years ago. It is now used to describe heritage, along with Latino and Latinx. One in three Americans says they have a close relative of another race. Many people have mixed backgrounds. This changes interactions in families and society.

American English has absorbed words and expressions from immigrant languages. More and more people, Latino or not, study Spanish in school. It is a big change from the mid-20th century, when people studied mostly French or German as a foreign language.

Each generation of arrivals in the United States has enriched American culture. Hamburgers, bagels, tacos, and, of course, pizza are now classic American foods. In 2015, Chinese restaurants outnumbered McDonald's, Burger King, and KFC restaurants combined! Other ethnic restaurants constantly spring up. Immigrant writers, movie makers, and other artists have added new themes to American culture. They have explored topics such as adjusting to life in America or the life of unauthorized immigrants. Musicians with Latin American roots have brought Latin rhythms to American genres.

Political scientists believe immigration has helped change election politics, as well. In 1980, more whites identified as Democrats than as Republicans. By 2010, it was the reverse. Concerns about immigration drew some working-class whites into the Republican camp. Surveys find that this group is worried about losing ground to the newcomers, economically and culturally. Republican politicians appeal to this concern with a promise to control immigration.

Economists say such fears are unjustified. They believe the presence of immigrant workers creates new job opportunities for U.S.-born workers. Foreign and U.S.-born workers often have different skills. They fill different types of jobs. As a result, they complement each other in the job market, rather than compete.

People who move to this country spend and invest their wages in the U.S. economy. It increases consumer demand and creates new jobs. Businesses respond to the presence of immigrant workers and consumers by expanding their operations in the United States, rather than overseas. Immigrants themselves frequently create new businesses. Nationwide, 1 in 5 business owners in 2014 was an immigrant. The ideas and innovations developed by these newcomers help grow the economy. Immigrants file patents at twice the rate of U.S.-born workers. They earn a larger share of advanced science and engineering degrees.

Immigrants have an outsized role in the U.S. high-tech industry—think Sergey Brin of Google or Eric Yuan, the Chinese-born founder of Zoom. In 2018, more than half of the 91 U.S. startup companies valued at $1 billion or more had at least

ZOOM IN: VIEWS OF IMMIGRATION

According to a Pew Research Institute study in 2021, the U.S. public is divided on immigration. Two-thirds of Americans (66 percent) say immigrants strengthen the country because of their hard work and talents. About one-fourth (24 percent) say immigrants burden the country by taking jobs, housing, and health care. These views vary by political affiliation. Among Democrats, 88 percent think immigrants strengthen the country. That number drops to 41 percent among Republicans. One-fourth of all Americans (24 percent) said legal immigration should be decreased. About one-third (38 percent) said it should be kept at its present level. Almost one-third (32 percent) said it should be increased.

one foreign-born founder. More than 80 percent of these companies employed immigrants in key management or research roles.

Service industries benefit a great deal from new arrivals, too. These workers can more easily fill essential roles, from picking crops to repairing houses to reducing shortages in health care professions. The COVID-19 pandemic showed how much the nation depends on essential workers. Immigrants made up 17 percent of grocery store clerks, 18 percent of food delivery drivers, and 19 percent of truck drivers. Foreign-born workers have a strong presence in health care jobs that require close contact with patients. They make up 17 percent of all workers, but 38 percent of home health aides, 29 percent of physicians, and 22 percent of nursing assistants. As the population ages, they will be even more critical to these occupations.

The impact of immigration on government budgets is uneven. Studies show that immigrants put more into federal programs than they take out. Unauthorized immigrants in particular pay taxes but are barred from collecting benefits. Still, the influx of people can put stress on state and local budgets.

Immigration can help solve these problems. It can fill labor gaps. It can increase the number of workers paying into Social Security.

Newcomers tend to be of working age. They are less likely to be children or retirees. The result is that they are actively contributing to programs such as Social Security, not taking money out of them. However, immigrants often have children using K-12 education. If the children are not already fluent in English, the costs to educate them may be higher than costs for U.S.-born children. This investment in children pays off later. But it can stress state and local budgets during the children's schooling.

The net cost to state and local budgets is closely related to education and income. For example, New Jersey has a high share of highly educated immigrants. By paying higher taxes, this group contributes more to the state budget than they consume in public services. In California, it is the opposite.

Social and economic trends suggest the need to reform the U.S. immigration system. The U.S population is aging. People over age 65 will outnumber children under age 18 by 2035. This will stress health care and Social Security programs. At the same time, the gap between labor needs and the skills of U.S.-born workers is expected to widen. The demand for workers in health care, hospitality, and other fields is expected to grow. The increasing education level of U.S.-born workers makes them less likely to fill these jobs.

Immigration can help solve these problems. It can fill labor gaps. It can increase the number of workers paying into Social Security. But political divisions make it difficult to make progress. Congress needs to work together to design a system that better serves the national interest. Immigration is a two-way process. As the nation embraces those seeking refuge and opportunity, it is in turn enriched by their energy, creativity, and dreams.

Getting Real

ERIC YUAN

When the COVID-19 pandemic began in 2020, life as most Americans knew it stopped. People went into lockdown mode, kept apart to help prevent the spread of disease. Seeing people and interacting with them was often an impossibility. Then came Zoom.

The Zoom app hosted work meetings, classes, parent-teacher conferences, even weddings. It helped millions of people communicate, work, and study during the pandemic. Zoom is the brainchild of an immigrant named Eric Yuan.

Originally from China, Yuan is the son of mining engineers. He studied math and computer science. He earned a master's degree in geology engineering. He became interested in videoconferencing because of long train rides to visit his girlfriend, who later became his wife.

Yuan was denied a work visa eight times before moving to California in 1997. He was inspired to try after hearing a talk by Microsoft founder Bill Gates about the possibilities of the Internet. He wanted to live in the country where the Internet was created and was growing the fastest. Yuan didn't know much English, but he was good at writing computer code. He started out as an engineer at Webex, a videoconferencing startup in California. He rose to become the vice president of engineering at Cisco, the computer networking company that acquired Webex in 2007. Yuan left Cisco in 2011 to create Zoom.

Yuan took Zoom public in April 2019. The app had impressed investors with its fast growth and profitability. As part of the COVID-19 response, Zoom worked with more than 100,000 school districts to deliver online education.

Today, Yuan is one of the world's 100 richest people.

KATYA ECHAZARRETA

On June 4, 2022, a Blue Origin rocket sent six people to the edge of outer space. Most of the travelers had paid a lot of money for their seats. But Katya Echazarreta was supported by an organization that sends exceptional leaders to space. Echazarreta is the first Mexican-born woman, and only the second Mexican, to travel to space.

When Echazarreta was seven years old, her family moved to the United States from Mexico. She recalls being overwhelmed by a new place. She did not speak the language. A teacher warned her she may be held back. Echazarreta told CNN reporters this "fueled" her.

When she was just a teenager, she "teamed up" with her single mom to raise her three siblings. To help support the family, she worked at McDonald's, as a dog walker, and as a grader for the community college she initially attended.

Echazarreta earned a bachelor's degree in electrical engineering from UCLA on a full scholarship. She interned at NASA's famed Jet Propulsion Laboratory and was offered a job as an electrical engineer. At the time of her space flight, she was completing her master's degree at Johns Hopkins University.

Echazarreta has a huge following on TikTok and hosts a science YouTube series. She is a presenter on the CBS TV show *Mission Unstoppable*. Her goal is to inspire others, especially Latinas and people of color, to achieve their dreams. "I would love to go to the moon," she said. "I'm going to see how I make it happen—but I'm going to make it happen."

Timeline

1790

The first U.S. census counts 3.9 million people. The British are the largest European group; 1 in 5 people are slaves.

1849

The first U.S. anti-immigrant political party, the "Know-Nothings," forms in reaction to Irish and German immigration.

1882

The Chinese Exclusion Act bars Chinese immigrants from entering the country.

1892

Ellis Island, the first U.S. immigration station, opens in New York Harbor.

1921

The Emergency Quota Act is the first law to set limits for immigration based on national origin.

1942

The United States and Mexico start the Bracero Program, which allows Mexican farm workers to enter the United States temporarily.

1952

The McCarran-Walter Act formally ends the exclusion of Asian immigrants to the United States.

1965

The Immigration and Nationality Act reorganizes the immigration system around the goals of reuniting families and filling labor needs.

1980

The Refugee Act creates a general policy for admission of refugees.

1986

The Simpson-Mazzoli Act grants amnesty to more than three million immigrants living illegally in the United States.

1990

The Immigration Act increases annual immigration caps and creates visas for temporary highly skilled and seasonal workers.

2006

The Secure Fence Act mandates the construction of a fence at the southern U.S. border.

2012

The Deferred Action for Childhood Arrivals (DACA) program begins. It shields those brought to the United States illegally as children from deportation.

2017

A ban on travel from several Muslim countries is imposed.

2018

A zero-tolerance policy begins, allowing for the arrest of anyone who crosses the southern border illegally.

2020

Asylum seekers at the southern border are turned away under a health emergency rule related to the COVID-19 pandemic.

2023

The COVID-19 health emergency expires. Asylum seekers from Cuba, Venezuela, Haiti, and other countries surge to the southern border.

Glossary

asylum seeker—a person seeking refuge in another country

census—an official count of a population

colony—a territory under the control of another country and occupied by settlers from that country

deport—to expel or banish a person from a country

famine—an extreme absence of food

green card—permission to live and work in the United States

immigrant—a person who comes to live permanently in a foreign country; a foreign-born resident

indentured servant—a person who exchanges years of free labor for travel or repayment of a loan

nativist—a person who believes in promoting the interests of native-born people over those of immigrants

persecution—ill treatment based on race, religion, or political beliefs

quota—a fixed minimum or maximum number

refugee—a person who has been forced to leave their country in order to escape war, persecution, or natural disaster

sanctuary—a place that has adopted policies friendly to immigrants, especially the unauthorized

visa—an official mark on a passport that allows the holder to enter, leave, or stay for a period of time

Selected Bibliography

Abramitzky, Ran, and Leah Boustan. *Streets of Gold: America's Untold Story of Immigrant Success*. New York: PublicAffairs, 2022.

Bon Tempo, Carl J., and Hasia R. Diner. *Immigration: An American History*. New Haven; London: Yale University Press, 2022.

Chomsky, Aviva. *"They Take Our Jobs!": And 20 Other Myths about Immigration*. Boston: Beacon Press, 2018.

Cornejo Villavicencio, Karla. *The Undocumented Americans*. New York: One World, 2020.

Foner, Nancy. *One Quarter of the Nation: Immigration and the Transformation of America*. Princeton: Princeton University Press, 2022.

Websites

American Immigration Council

https://www.americanimmigrationcouncil.org/topics/history-immigration

This non-partisan site includes fact sheets, reports, blogs, and more related to the history of immigration in the United States.

Carnegie Corporation of New York

https://www.carnegie.org/our-work/article/15-myths-about-immigration-debunked

Learn the truth behind a few immigration myths.

Migration Policy Institute

https://www.migrationpolicy.org/article/frequently-requested-statistics-immigrants-and-immigration-united-states

Review historic U.S. immigration trends.

Index